# Kris Kringle: Santa Claus from Man to Myth

Chris Gay

Gay, Christopher

Suesea Press

Manchester, Connecticut

The Passion of the Chris, LLC

Notice of Liability

ISBN 978-0-9844673-2-7

www.chrisjgay.com

# ALSO BY CHRIS GAY

## Novels

Ghost of a Chance

## Novella

Sherlock Holmes and the Final Reveal

## Humor

The Bachelor Cookbook: Edible Meals with a Side of Sarcasm

And That's the Way It Was…Give or Take: A Daily Dose of My
Radio Writings

Shouldn't Ice Cold Beer Be Frozen? My 365 Random Thoughts to
Improve Your Life Not One Iota

Another Round of Ice Cold Beer: My 365 More Random Thoughts
to Improve You're Life Not One Iota.

# DEDICATION

To my nephew Jaeden, and to all who'll never outgrow the Spirit of Christmas.

"He who has not Christmas in his heart will never find it under a tree."
-Roy L. Smith

# AUTHOR'S NOTE

While I've tried to be as accurate as possible with history and geography, some measure of adjustment, along with literary license, was necessary to better flavor the story. But hey, this is a biography of a fictional character. I'm sure you'll do well with it.
-Christopher

# FOREWORD

Tales of Santa Claus have been told and re-told many times, of course. And while numerous versions have been recounted, this book presents his actual origin tale in its entirety. This is the story of how Kristopher Nicholas Kringle, a virtuous, ordinary, 18th Century New England man, became one of our culture's most revered and iconic figures. From his humble Connecticut start, all the way to his historic first Christmas Eve sleigh ride, it's all here-with a little humor sprinkled in. This is a Christmas story that can be enjoyed by anyone, on any day, throughout every season. So, no matter what day of the year it is as you read these words, Merry Christmas.

# PROLOGUE

Jacob Kringle was a successful 18th Century west coast gold
prospector who hailed from New England. He was born in
1746 to Andrew and Mary Kringle at Hartford, in the British
colony of Connecticut. Jacob was raised at the family homestead in
South Windsor, where in 1772 he married his wife, Cupid. After
their wedding they moved twenty miles east to Coventry, in
Windham County.

Upon reaching mid-life he found himself well-situated, and the
thanks for that went to his oldest friend, Nathaniel Donner. Donner
was a remarkably benevolent man. Indeed, it was he who had
raced Jacob home through a powerful Nor'Easter in his horse-
driven sleigh on Christmas Eve of 1776. That enormous effort
allowed Jacob to make it to Cupid's bedside just in time for the
birth of his son, whom they named Kristopher.

As the Kringle's produced no further offspring, Donner's
selflessness and disregard for his own safety had bestowed upon
Jacob an irreplaceable gift. His noble act left Kringle owing Nate a
debt of gratitude that he could never possibly repay. Donner
refused to acknowledge that debt in any event, and his generosity
to Jacob's family still wasn't finished.

Shortly after Kris was born Nate Donner, a widower, left his
Connecticut home to Jacob's indefinite care to explore what lay
beyond the western border of the American Colonies; even to as
far out as the Pacific Ocean. It was the act of a true pioneer,

coming nearly thirty years before Thomas Jefferson commissioned Meriwether Lewis and William Clark to do the same thing. Donner knew attempting such a trip would at times be perilous. He was not wrong.

The only thing that gave Donner pause was that the American Revolution had begun in earnest. However, few observers thought it would, or even could, last very long. It was simply not possible that the highly-inexperienced Colonials could accomplish the unprecedented feat of winning their independence from the massive world power that was England. He chose to go ahead with his trip.

After months of traveling across the land, Donner reached the California territory. His four-plus years spent in the shadow of the Pacific had met with great success. By early spring of 1781 he had secured his financial future and decided to return home to Connecticut.

Sparing no expense, he hired the most experienced guides he could find to assist in returning him home safely. The trip was successful; they reached Coventry on November 1st. And so, Nate arrived on Jacob Kringle's doorstep a mere fortnight after British General Charles Cornwallis surrendered to his American counterpart, George Washington, at Yorktown, Virginia. An act that shocked the world and, for all intents and purposes, ended the Revolutionary War.

After welcoming back his old friend, Jacob informed him that, aside from the formalities, the Revolution was over. The Colonies he'd returned to would be an independent nation.

Jacob, Nate and Cupid celebrated well into the night. Kris, who was only months-old when his de facto uncle left New England, was now nearly five. Cupid re-introduced them, and Kris politely told Mr. Donner that it was very nice to meet him. He then went back to playing with his favorite toys; wooden ships that Jacob had hand-carved for him.

After dinner the trio got around to discussing the full story of Donner's time out west. Nate told about how he had, quite inadvertently, discovered a quantity of gold in a shallow stream he'd forded near the Spanish fort of San Francisco. Donner was adamant there was more and, as if to prove it, took a solid gold nugget out of his pocket. He placed it into the palm of a stunned Jacob Kringle and told him to keep it. After dismissing Jacob's protests, Nate finished his interesting tale. Afterward, he suggested the Kringle's take their own California trip to try and secure their finances, too. Jacob replied with sincerity that he would consider it. By the time Nate finally rose to leave it was after 4 a.m. Jacob handed Nate his old house keys, and they vowed to get together frequently.

Unfortunately, those plans, as well as Donner's dream of building himself a new homestead, never came to fruition. He would not have long to enjoy the fruits of his explorations, as just a short time later he took ill and passed away. In his will, aside from a modest amount given to Jacob, Donner's remaining estate was left to his elderly parents.

In July of 1782, the Kringle's moved west to seek the fortune their friend had found- sixty-seven years before the storied flood of '49ers would. After arriving Jacob kept Nate's extensive advice and instructions in mind at all times. And good fortune was with them in California too, as within a single year of gold prospecting he'd panned enough of the precious metal to build his family a sizable house.

Reclusive and independent by nature, and now with the means to be even more so, he decided to build far away from any organized settlements. To start the process, Jacob left his family behind briefly to scout out suitable land. He headed north with four hired guides to the Russian territory of Alaska. And it was there, barely inside the Arctic Circle, that he'd found just the spot he was looking for. It was within the tree line, (there comes a point up north at which temperatures are too cold for trees to grow) close to the Arctic Ocean, and plentiful with caribou. After carefully logging its position he returned to San Francisco. There he hired a team of carpenters and purchased the materials required to construct his homestead, which he would christen "Snowhenge". Then he and his team headed back to the Arctic to build it. Upon its completion, Jacob sent for his family to join him. Two of the carpenters, with no families to return to, agreed to stay on and work as live-in handymen.

As the years wore on, the Kringle's and their pair of employees lived well off the land. Jacob taught his son to fish, hunt and survive the elements. In the summer of 1796, nineteen year-old Kris told his parents that he was leaving the homestead. He would first go south to what would later become the Oregon Territory, and then east from there. Although Cupid was distraught at the news, Jacob had always understood that this time would come. That was simply the way of the world. What did surprise Jacob though was when in 1799 his son returned home, and not alone. In the three years he'd been gone Kris had courted and married the former Catherine Flake.

Kris told of how he'd met Cathy while making his way east along the Clearwater River near what is now Lewiston, Idaho. Cathy was from northern Ohio, the daughter of two settlers who'd gone west from Rhode Island. Ironically, her area of Ohio was part of Connecticut until just a few years previous. So technically, though separated by almost six hundred miles, for a time both she and Kris had called the same Colony home.

After both her parents passed away Cathy, who had no other kin, decided to take what little money she'd been left with and, like Nathaniel Donner before her, try the risky move westward with her sights set on Oregon. She'd hired two guides, and the trio carefully made their way toward the Pacific. They traveled through southern South Dakota, northern Nebraska and Wyoming before attaining Idaho. When they reached the Clearwater River her party opted to set up camp and rest for a few weeks. It was along the banks of that river, while her guides were teaching her to fish, that Kris had come along.

She didn't look to be much of a fisherman, and while walking by Kris made a joke about it. She'd laughed and invited him to join them for lunch. He accepted only on the condition that he be allowed to help procure that day's rations. Owing to his years of training on the Artic Ocean, Kris was a superb fisherman. Within a few hours he had caught three days' worth of meals for them all. She thanked him profusely, and after dinner they went for a walk that included a nice conversation. Kris ended up camping with her party that night, and for a few nights after as well.

By the end of the second week there was no denying that they were falling in love. On a perfect, cloudless evening on the same bank of the Clearwater River on which they'd first met, Kris proposed, and Cathy accepted. The next day Cathy asked her guides if they would do her the honor of attending the wedding, both out of respect and due to the friendship they'd developed over their time together. Having become as fond of her as she was of them, they readily agreed. Cathy also informed both that after the wedding she would pay her remaining obligation on their Oregon contract in full, and then dissolve it.

On July 16, 1797 at a meeting house in Nez Perce County, Idaho, Kristopher Nicholas Kringle and Catherine Susan Flake were married by a local minister.

After their small wedding Kris offered to backtrack west so they could, at least temporarily, settle in San Francisco. Aside from Connecticut and the Arctic, it was the only area of which he had much knowledge about. Cathy thought that to be a great idea and so west to San Francisco they went, and then stayed, for two years. In October of 1799 Kris asked Cathy if she would like to meet her in-laws in the Arctic Circle. Without hesitation she answered that she'd be delighted. And so that was how it came to be that in November 1799 Mr. and Mrs. Kringle arrived at the Alaskan homestead of Mr. and Mrs. Kringle.

Jacob and Cupid were ecstatic to see their son and meet their new daughter-in-law. They welcomed them into their home for as long as they might wish to stay. During Kris's time away Jacob had expanded the house, and added a livery stable for the caribou. The former action allowed plenty of space for everyone. Much to Kris's great surprise, Cathy took well to both the weather and lifestyle. And so, what was meant to be a two-month stay instead turned into a permanent living arrangement. Jacob and Cupid occupied one half of the house; Kris and Cathy, the other.

Over the next few years Cathy learned the ways of the Arctic. This included how to work their primary form of transportation, a sleigh driven by Jacob Kringle's domesticated caribou. She called them her "reindeer."

They bonded well as a family. That included the handymen, Charlie and William, who were still there; each playing his own part to keep the estate running smoothly. They ate meals together every night, and every Sunday ended with the singing of songs; accompanied by piano music performed by the truly gifted William.

This went on regularly until 1809, when they lost Cupid. The atmosphere of good humor was never quite the same after, and in 1813 Jacob joined his beloved wife at peace. Before succumbing he called Kris to his bedside. Jacob expressed his pride in him, and told him what a great son he had been and always would be. The father then asked the son if he'd planned on staying after he passed. Kris told him yes and informed him that he'd already spoken to William and Charlie, who both agreed to remain in their positions as well.

Upon hearing that, Jacob broke into a smile. He knew Snowhenge would be well taken care of by Kris and Cathy. He felt at peace, and two days after that conversation the family patriarch went to his eternal rest. At the age of thirty-six, Kris was now head of the household. And he vowed to never let Cathy or his parents down.

# 1821

1

K ris Kringle trudged slowly through the ever-deepening January snow. Each laborious step was another challenge to merely keep his balance. His task was made more difficult by a combination of the driving precipitation and cold winds whipping off the Arctic Ocean. Still, he was now less than a quarter mile from Snowhenge and the conditions were by no means foreign to him. As such, he was prepared. Not including the sack resting upon his back, his forest-green parka was only the last of the five layers of clothing he was wearing. The heavy coat's fur-lined hood was pulled tightly over his head. All that showed of him was a small tuft of fiery-red hair, flaked with gray, which stuck out and crested over the top of his forehead. Another quarter-hour passed and, just as he was able to see the outline of his home through the relentless blizzard, a familiar figure came into view. It was Nutmeg, his oldest and most trusted reindeer. Kringle veered over toward him and took hold of his reins.

He shouted into the blustery wind, "What's the matter, old buddy; think I couldn't get back without a guide?" Kringle held on to him, and together they started walking to the house. "I'm only forty-four, Nutty. I've still got a lot of mileage left in these legs."

Nutmeg turned his head slightly to his long-time master and

offered a look of amusement that, if ol' Kris Kringle didn't know better, he would've sworn included a sarcastic eye-roll.

They trudged ahead until, at last, they'd made it back to the homestead, where they were met by a worried-looking Cathy.

"Where have you been, Nicky?!" She nearly always called him by his middle name, and had since even in the short time before they were married. "What on Earth possessed you to go out in this weather?"

Kris stepped inside the doorway as Nutmeg wandered off toward the livery. Once indoors, he began the arduous task of removing the top four layers.

"Honey, I'm fine. I just had to run an errand is all."

"In a blizzard?"

"I had no choice, it had to be today."

"Why today?"

"Because it's our anniversary."

"Sweetheart, our anniversary is in July."

"No Catherine, our *wedding* anniversary is in July. Today's the anniversary of us deciding to stay here at Snowhenge and make a life for ourselves. As it turned out, aside from marrying you it was the best decision I've ever made. Why not mark the occasion?"

"Oh, my goodness! You're a Saint, Nick."

"I wouldn't go that far. But I do love you." He took the red sack he'd been carrying and from it removed a gift. It was neatly wrapped, and sported a large green bow. He handed it to her. "Happy 21st Cathy."

"But I didn't get you anything."

"Where would you? There isn't a store to be found for hundreds of miles."

"Then where did you get this?" She asked, holding up the box.

"A man has his secrets too, Catherine. Open it," he said with a smile.

Cathy carefully unwrapped the package and laid the paper down neatly on a nearby end-table. She then opened it and revealed a diamond snowflake pendant attached to a silver chain.

"Oh, my goodness, Nicky. You shouldn't have."

"Why not? It's beautiful, you're beautiful. Sounds like a good match to me."

She leaned over and hugged him tightly as tears ran down her cheeks. "Thank you so much…I'll put it on right now." As she did she took a moment to admire it in the hallway mirror.

"Is there any food? I'm starving," Kris asked as he pulled off his boots.

"Plenty. You didn't really think *I* forgot this anniversary, did you? I've been preparing a special dinner for tonight."

"You're the best,' he replied with affection.

"I'd say we're equal."

He left it at that and headed into the kitchen to see what was on that evening's menu. What he saw was enough fare for a king's banquet. And when dinner was ready they enjoyed a hearty feast, after which they reminisced while relaxing in each other's company.

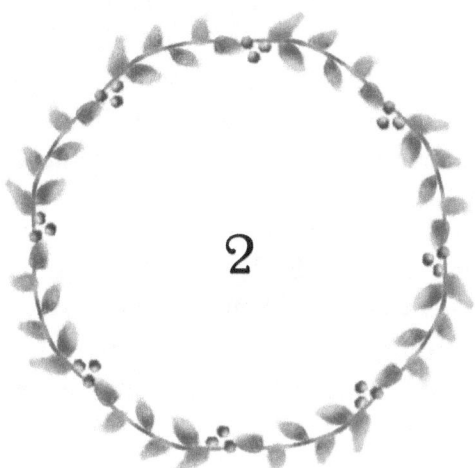

2

The next day was Sunday, and no one in the household felt much like doing anything. Up in the Arctic Circle there were no neighbors, shops or restaurants. There were precious few entertainment options aside from one's own hobbies, which were generally cultivated from some talent learned during youth and mastered gradually over the ensuing years.

Like his father before him, Kris Kringle's skill was whittling. With just his pocket knife and some time he could transform a simple block of wood into a majestic ship that, if not for its size, could scarcely be told from a real one. It was on Sundays, with minimal chores to attend to and the opportunity to just sit by the fire and whittle, that he allowed himself to pay attention to his more idle thoughts. Such as that, perhaps, he was meant for something greater. Maybe even have a chance to someday give back to the world that had provided so much to him and his family.

It was these thoughts that he once again pondered while in his easy chair, ready to take on the task born of an idea he'd recently had: a sculpture depicting a wooden ship inside a wooden bottle. To his right, the flames flickered in the fireplace over the cracks and pops of the wood they were steadily consuming. Outside the large bay window in front of him Kris could see that the snow had picked up its pace and was now coming down at the speed of rain. He was silently grateful that he'd be spending the day inside, away from the elements and enveloped in warmth and comfort.

Kris sat back with his wedge of timber and began to make the first cuts into it. As each incision was completed, a curled wood shaving fell away and onto the floor. A few landed on his shoes. After a short time a small pile began to form as the bottle started to take shape. His concentration increased as the work became more precise. Kris's vision still held firm at 20/20, which helped greatly when etching in the finer details of a wood carving.

As he was rounding off an edge, Cathy came in carrying a cup of tea. Wisps of steam emanated from it and then spiraled upward before dissipating. Kris, having lost himself in his work, took no notice.

"Here you are, Nicky," Cathy said tenderly as she placed the cup and saucer down on the small end table next to him.

"Oh, thank you, honey," he said upon hearing her voice.

"My goodness look at that snow come down," she observed. "I haven't seen it like this in quite some time."

Kris stopped whittling and laid his carving knife on the table. "No, I can't say that I have either. In fact if this weren't Sunday, I don't think we'd even..." Kris's words trailed off as he looked up again through the window. "Whatever in the world? Is there someone out there?"

Cathy took a closer look out into the driving snow and squinted through her spectacles, but her eyesight wasn't as good as her husband's. "I don't see anything, Nicky. Are you su–wait! Yes, I believe you're right."

In the distance they could make out a speck of red that grew larger and more distinct the closer it got. Soon they both could see the outline of a man coming toward their house. He was dressed in a thick red parka with white trim, white gloves, black pants and a red cap beneath the parka's hood.

"But that's impossible," Cathy exclaimed softly. "He has no sleigh, no animals. How could anyone walk out here; and from where?"

"Theoretically, yes. It would seem almost impossible," he responded. "Yet there he is." Kris stood up from his chair and brushed away the wood shavings that had clung to him. "Well, it looks like we have a guest. I'll let him in."

He walked out of the parlor room and toward the vestibule with Cathy following close behind. Just as he got to the door, their brass knocker sounded from the other side. Kris briefly looked back at his wife, and they exchanged puzzled glances. He then turned and reached out for the door knob.

3

**K**ristopher Nicholas Kringle?" The man at his door shouted from the front step over the din of the weather. It was more of a statement than a question.

"Yes, I am he. Please, won't you come in?"

"Thank you, sir." The newcomer kicked the excess snow from his boots and stepped inside the foyer. Kris closed the door behind him and they were instantly cut off from the elements. "May I hang up my coat?"

"Of course," said Cathy. "Please sir, give it over to me and I'll hang it up to dry."

"Excellent. You're very kind, Ma'am." With that he removed it and handed it over. Both Kringles were startled to see that he was wearing nothing more than a white dress shirt under his parka, though neither of them made mention of it. Around his neck was an impeccably-knotted, solid red bowtie.

He extended his hand toward Kris, who shook it. "My name is Gregory Blitzen, Mr. Kringle. It's so good to finally meet you and your lovely wife."

"Likewise, I'm sure," Cathy answered politely. She then reached into the hall closet for a hanger, draped the parka on it, and hung it from one of several hooks that extended down from the foyer's ceiling.

"Yes, likewise, Mr. Blitzen." Kris began. "However…" Blitzen interrupted.

"I'm sure you have many questions, sir. And I'll be happy to answer them all to the best of my ability. For the moment though is there a place that we three may sit and talk?"

"Certainly. Let's move into my parlor. You'll have to excuse the wood shavings about the room, Mr. Blitzen. Whittling is my Sunday hobby and I'm afraid we weren't expecting any company today.

"Not at all," Blitzen said as they walked. Once there Kris motioned him to a comfortably overstuffed chair that was mostly reserved for the rare guests they entertained. Both Kris and Cathy sat down on the room's couch, facing him.

"May I get you some refreshments, Mr. Blitzen?" She inquired. "You must be starving after your journey. Or at the very least thirsty."

"No ma'am, I'm fine thank you. I don't wish to put you to any inconvenience."

"It's really no…" She began.

"It's all right," he repeated. Then he turned to look at Kris. "Now then, Mr. Kringle. I have come to speak with you about a matter of some importance."

"Shall I leave you two alone to converse?" Cathy asked.

"No. In fact I'd much prefer it if you would stay, Mrs. Kringle. This concerns you, too."

"All right then, Mr. Blitzen," Cathy's husband cut in. "What may we do for you? And please, call me "Kris". This is a very informal household."

"Indeed it is. And in that same spirit of informality please call me "Greg". Now as I was saying Kris, there is a matter I'd like to discuss. Or to be more specific, an opportunity." Blitzen saw the confusion etched clearly on their faces, and quickly went on. "You have led an exemplary life; you and Cathy both."

"How could you possibly know anything about our lives?" A

bewildered Kris managed to say.

"I know all about both of you. If truth be told, I know much about a great many people."

"If I may beg your pardon Mr. Blitzen, just who are you?" Cathy probed.

"It's "Greg". Please. Who I am is really not much more than a glorified representative."

"Of whom?"

Blitzen disregarded her question and looked at her husband. "Kris, may I be so intrusive and tactless as to ask you what your beliefs are?"

"Don't you know already?" Kringle answered, for the first time with a hint of irritation.

"Well, let's just say I'd like to hear it directly from you." Blitzen could tell some form of reassurance was needed. "Listen, you both saw how I arrived here; how I was dressed. And frankly the parka was more for show than anything else until I could introduce myself. I mean you no difficulties. As I've said I'm here simply to present an opportunity, and then I'll do what I can to answer your questions. Please rest assured that I have come to you both in earnest."

Kris considered this and recognized the obvious truth in his words. It certainly couldn't hurt to hear the man out. Besides, his curiosity had certainly been peaked.

"Okay, Greg. We may continue. As to your question, I'm not quite certain what I believe in. Are you saying that there is, in fact, an actual deity?"

Greg Blitzen smiled. "I haven't yet said anything on the subject. But I will answer you with this." He paused briefly. Not so much for effect, but more to signal them both that what was coming next was decidedly worth their undivided attention.

"Many people the world over believe in different gods and different religions. Some don't believe in anything. And like you, some simply aren't sure. So who's right, then? And who's wrong? If you're a good person, if you treat others well and respect humanity, then it doesn't really matter. Though I'll confirm for you with certainty what does exist: Nature. And from it all things in this world come. Undoubtedly Kris your next question is, was Nature itself created by an all-powerful deity? And my answer to you is maybe, or maybe not. Please understand that to confirm a deity would deny you forevermore the common tenet which exists throughout all religions: faith. And the denial of faith is something no true God would ever tolerate. However to confirm that no deity exists ahead of time, if indeed there is none, would throw off the natural schedule of Science and the further discovery of its workings that Nature has put into place."

"Talk about hedging your bets," Kris Kringle said after absorbing what he'd just heard.

"Again, you saw how I came to you. Was it magic? Well if magic exists it too comes from Nature, Kris. And sometimes what is perceived as "magic" is merely science that has not yet been understood."

"All right, I see your point. And I don't mind saying that it's one I'll spend a good share of my time reflecting upon. So now let's speak on the matter of your visit. You mentioned an opportunity of some kind?"

"Indeed, I did. Allow me to present it to you."

"By all means." Kris threw a quick glance toward Cathy, who didn't notice. She appeared to be fully captivated by the content of their guest's speech.

"Thank you. Now, I am aware of your history. You were born in what is now the American state of Connecticut on Christmas Eve 1776, less than six months after the founding of your country. While still a child your father moved your family west where he prospered enough to build the residence in which we currently sit, and which later became yours by way of inheritance upon his passing in 1813. In 1796 you set out on your own and in 1797 married Catherine Flake in what will become, 69 years hence, the American state of Idaho. After which in 1799 you both returned here, where you eventually decided to take up permanent residence while assisting your parents. You've honored your late father's wishes to maintain this homestead, and you've kept employed as handymen men who'd otherwise have nowhere else to go. And more than that, you've treated them as family. While they were alive, you'd always respected your parents. When on your own, both before and after meeting Cathy, you treated all who you knew and all who you met with compassion, benevolence, and charity, with no thought of recompense or even recognition of any kind whatsoever. On one occasion not long after leaving Snowhenge, having not eaten yourself in two full days, you were finally able to earn enough to purchase some bread and meat. Shortly thereafter you happened upon another man whom you correctly perceived to be in dire need of sustenance, more so than even yourself. As such, you gave him your entire dinner. And when he offered you some back to share, you refused to take even a small portion."

Cathy looked over toward her husband with love in her eyes. "You've never told me about that, Nicky."

"It was of no consequence."

"Oh, but that's very much untrue, Kris Kringle. On the contrary it is of great consequence." Blitzen looked at Cathy. "No Ma'am, he didn't tell you that. Nor any of a hundred other stories of a similar nature. As good a man as you think your husband to be, and I know how much that is, he is an even better man than that. In fact substantially better. Is that not so, Kris?"

"I honestly prefer not to talk about it. If I'm made aware of someone in need and I can help him, I will. Accolades mean nothing to me. In fact they'd mean less than nothing, if that were possible."

"But don't you see? That is exactly what makes you special. And it's why I'm here today. Understand that every deed we perform, both good and bad, no matter how seemingly inconsequential, is documented. Though not unprecedented, your attitude toward your fellow man is extraordinary. And it is tops among all humans who currently exist. The reality is that some things in life are truly about timing. And right now, in the overall scheme of things, your timing is very good."

"Timing for what? What do you have in mind?"

Greg Blitzen reached down and picked up a handful of wood shavings from the floor, then leaned back.

"You are good with whittling, I see." He looked around the

room, where various finished carvings adorned the fireplace mantle, windowsills and end tables. "These sculptures you've created are truly exquisite."

"They're all right. As I've said, it's more of a hobby than anything else."

"Perhaps. Tell me, though. Have you ever thought that maybe there's a greater purpose for you in this world?"

Kris Kringle's face went pale. *How could this man possibly know my very thoughts*? He wondered. Before he could answer, Blitzen continued on as if he'd already had.

"Yes, I think so. Well I'm here to offer you the chance to realize that purpose. If, that is, you wish to go forward with that sentiment."

"Yes, of course. But how?"

"These are not the best of times, Kris. And the world has become in short supply of one of humanity's greatest unseen necessities: *Hope*. Many have simply lost hope, I'm afraid. And once lost it's a very difficult thing to retrieve. With that said, we believe the best way to go about instilling hope is through young people. To show them the virtues of kindness and charity at the very start, in the hope that as they grow older they'll remember just how important those virtues are. When people coming into this world with little-to-nothing are provided with items that bring them happiness, that feeling of joy stays with them throughout their lifetimes. In both good times and in bad those memories remain frozen; cherished. And they're perhaps what they may even lean on during hard times in their adulthoods. Too, should they become prosperous, those reminiscences may very well be what leads them to provide for others the way they themselves had been provided for. Does this make sense to you?"

"It does." Kris responded. His voice was distant. His face, contemplative.

"It seems that there is yet more you wish to say on the matter, Greg," Cathy interjected.

"Yes, ma'am. There is. We also believe that this gesture of goodwill should be centralized around a time of year at which benevolent attitudes are already amplified throughout both the secular and religious alike. This would greatly augment its positive impact."

"Do you have a specific period of time in mind?" Kris queried.

"Christmas," he answered candidly. "You see Kris, Hope is *my* department, and it's my job to see that it gets restored. There is really no better time of year to promote hope -as well as faith- in your fellow man. Not to mention the many ancillary acts of altruism that generally accompany such sentimentalities. And so now I'm asking you, would you like to be a part of this?"

Despite feeling overwhelmed by all that had just been told to him, Kris Kringle maintained his outwardly calm demeanor. And still there was the matter of finding out what any of this had to do with him.

"I think you already know that I can't answer that question just yet, Greg. Not until I ask one of my own."

"Where do you fit in?"

"Yes. What have I to do with these plans you've described?"

"You would manufacture a variety of toys here on-site year 'round for all of the young people worldwide, and then distribute them over the course of a single night."

"Impossible," Kris and Cathy both replied in unison.

Gregory Blitzen sighed. "Do you both honestly believe that I would be here now if it was? I realize that the concept is difficult to grasp, but please trust in me when I tell you that it is, in fact, doable."

"Fair enough," said Kris, and left it at that. "What night, incidentally?"

"December 24th."

"My birthday. Now there's a coincidence."

"Kris, not everything in life that appears to be coincidental in reality is." Blitzen leaned forward in his chair and looked Kris Kringle directly in the eyes to ensure he had his complete attention. "Now then, you would need to build an expansion onto this house to serve as your factory. You would also have to train your stable of caribou to fly."

"To fl-"

"Yes, to fly. You'd need a team of eight caribou ready and capable of maintaining a demanding, rigorous flight schedule every Christmas Eve. This means that your entire herd would be taught so that there would be multiple substitutes for each member of the main team in the event of unforeseen circumstances. Now, then. The caribou will be instructed in all facets of the subject. And to increase their skills and endurance they will participate in a series of seasonal, for lack of a better term, "reindeer games". On December 24$^{th}$ your strongest eight will be harnessed and attached to a large sleigh, which you will then drive through the night sky around the globe. The delivery of your gifts will be completed prior to sunrise on Christmas Day. Too, you must agree to stay here in the Arctic away from the public and anyone else, save for your handymen. The only acceptable correspondence with the outside world would be through the post or what you'll soon come to know as the *telegraph*. Late in the 20$^{th}$ Century, that'll be expanded to a medium that will be christened *electronic mail*, and later still through your *official website.* As you may have already surmised in exchange, and frankly out of necessity, the lifespans of both you and Cathy will be significantly extended. Now, you're both American citizens and will officially remain as such. Therefore you will reside permanently in America. However in reality, you will become a citizen of the entire world."

"We're in Russian territory here Greg, not American," Cathy offered.

"That is true, at the present time. However approximately five decades hence Russia will sell Alaska to the United States, where it will remain an American territory until it eventually becomes your 49$^{th}$ state in the year 1959. Now, are there any more questions before I proceed?"

Kris's head was swimming with the incredible amount of data he was being presented with, and hardly knew where to begin with his questions. After a moment of thinking it over he decided to start with the practical. "Mr. Blitzen, it's not that I'm adverse to the idea, you understand. But I'm forty-four years of age. While that's not old to be sure, it's not young enough to handle all of what you've asked. Even if I was able to enlist Chuck and Billy to help me with all of that, there'd be no way to maintain even the regular upkeep of Snowhenge itself. And that's not even addressing the inarguable fact that I have absolutely no idea how to teach a reindeer to fly."

Blitzen paused a moment before responding, and then asked, "Kris Kringle, are you familiar with the word *elf?*"

"Elf?" Kris repeated it while thinking over the query. "That is some sort of sprite, is it not? A fictional entity, slight in size with mystical abilities; referenced mostly in children's literature?"

Blitzen laughed. "Well, you're partially correct. All you've stated is true with the exception that they are not fictional, their existence is very much a reality. And like me, they too exist to serve Nature and/or Nature's Creator. Should you opt to accept this obligation, three hundred elves will join you and work under your stewardship. They can build anything, including but not limited to the factory extension on this house and their own living quarters. Upon that project's completion, they'll spend their workdays constructing a variety of toys. And each time you see fit to complete an original wood carving they'll duplicate it exactly, thousands of times over. This will not only allow you to continue practicing your hobby, but also to provide another choice of toy to go out every year. In addition, animal-training elves will teach your reindeer to both fly and communicate with you. They'll also supervise the reindeer games. All of the elves will report to you, and you will determine which are best suited for which tasks." You can participate as much or as little as you'd like with regard to carving toys and running the factory. But your primary responsibility, aside from your annual flight of course, will be mainly to supervise the operation." Blitzen went quiet, and sat back in his chair.

Kris turned to Cathy, and they looked at each other in silence for a moment. Then Cathy broke it. "Well, Nicky. It would be a chance to do some real good, *and* allow us to spend more time together than we ever thought possible. To be honest that's just as important to me, if not even more so."

"Yes, of course. It's just that this is all coming at me so fast, honey," he said to her. Kris Kringle then regarded their guest. "I suppose that once my decision is made it is irrevocable." Greg nodded to indicate that was indeed the case.

"It's now early January, so if we do this we'd have nearly an entire year to get everything up and running by next Christmas."

"That is not coincidental either, Mr. Kringle. If you accept, you may tell your handymen tonight, and tomorrow the elves will arrive. If you decline, I must move on to the next man in line for the job."

"Who did you contact before me?"

"No one. You were at the top of my list."

"Really?"

"Yes. I checked it twice."

"I see."

"However, I will need your answer by the end of this day."

"Yes, well…" Kris glanced at Cathy once more, and then over to the fireplace. The flames were still crackling along as vividly as they had been earlier. He stared at them for a good long while. All conversation had ceased and the room went completely still. Finally at long last, and without taking his eyes off the burning logs, he spoke.

"There are many ways in which a man might look upon an opportunity such as this, Mr. Blitzen. In the interest of time I won't name them all, but I will tell you which way I've decided to view it. To be the first man in recorded history called upon to create and oversee such an awesome initiative is humbling to a degree which I cannot express in mere words. I hope that those I've just used are sufficient enough to convey my appreciation. As far as my answer to you, Greg…I accept."

"Outstanding," Blitzen said through a huge smile as he stood up and extended his hand.

Kris and Cathy also stood together, the latter's face beaming with silent joy. Kris reached out and shook Greg's hand. And just like that, it was done.

"Need I sign anything?"

"No, nothing at all. With us your word is quite good enough.

Now, before we proceed there are a few more details you need to know. Blitzen returned to his seat, and that seemed to be his hosts' cue to return to theirs. The follow-up conversation ended up lasting well into the evening.

4

The next morning Kris and Cathy Kringle's new life began without fanfare, and the day itself started out similar to the thousands of others that had preceded it. Cathy was brewing tea while Kris retrieved a pair of teacups and saucers from the cupboard. They were both a little sluggish; neither had gotten much sleep.

Greg Blitzen hadn't left until nearly eight o'clock. After seeing him out, Kris called William and Charlie into the parlor. He told them a condensed version of the story, then asked if they'd wanted to be a part of this new life. Kris wasn't surprised at all when they both agreed without hesitation. Charlie asked how they'd be able to maintain their anonymity, even in the Arctic, once the Kringle's became a household name. That was one of the supplemental questions Kris himself had asked Greg, and he reiterated the answer. Their location would be cloaked to the eyes of all who were not part of Snowhenge; which to the rest of the world would henceforth be known simply as *The North Pole*. The reality though was that, while they were indeed very far north, Snowhenge was nowhere near the North Pole. And there was no way they could be anyway, as the real North Pole lay under the Arctic Ocean and its ever-transient ice sheets. However, most people didn't know such things, and it also served to throw off-track all who might seek their actual location.

That lone query comprised the entirety of their questions. They'd thanked him, then returned to their respective quarters.

And that was that.

Cathy had just begun pouring tea, when for the second straight day there was a knock at the door.

"I'll get it," Kris said and left the kitchen. On his way to the foyer he glanced through a window and out onto what looked to be a milder day. There was no snow to be seen that wasn't already on the ground.

He opened the door to find a small man standing upon his step. He stood around four feet in height, and was dressed in a noticeably untailored suit of clothes. He wore a dark blue suit-coat over a vest, along with a white linen shirt. Attached to the vest was a gold pocket watch, and around his neck was a blue cravat. It appeared to have been hastily tied, and with all the care that a cow might demonstrate while choosing a pair of socks. Atop his head sat a plain woolen cap, from either side of which two pointed ears protruded. Taken all together, he was a rather comical sight.

"May I help you?"

"I'm looking for a Kristopher Kringle, sir. Would you be him?"

"I would be. And to whom am I addressing?"

"The name's Graham. Mr. Blitzen sent me. I'm an elf, here to help get your new venture up and running."

"Of course, Graham. A pleasure. I was expecting that there would be others with you."

"Oh, they'll be 'round soon enough. They're collecting the wood we'll be using to build this compound. I came on ahead to introduce myself and get your orders on a few things upfront."

"I see. Won't you come in then? I was just about to join my

wife for tea."

"Thank you." Graham kicked one shoe against the other in turn to shake them free of excess snow, then stepped inside.

In the kitchen Kris introduced Graham to Cathy, and she poured him a cup of tea as well.

"I thank you, ma'am." He pulled himself up onto a chair that was much too large for him. Once sat however, it appeared that despite his size he fit at the table comfortably. Graham reached over, picked up the sugar bowl and added two teaspoons of its contents into his cup. He gave the tea exactly four swirls with the spoon, removed it from the saucer, and then finished the entire cup in one swig. "Excellent, ma'am. Much obliged, I'm sure."

"You're welcome," Cathy returned with a warm smile.

"Now then, Kris Kringle," he said while pulling an old, worn notebook out of his suit pocket. Shall we get on with it?"

Kris laughed. "I can see you're eager."

"There's lots to go over before the rest of the elves get here, and a few decisions I need you to make."

"Certainly. Been doing this awhile, have you?"

"I'd say so. I'm 389 years old."

"Is that so? Well Graham you don't look a day over 388, ho-ho-ho," Kris chuckled.

"Joke, is it? Guess I'd better get used to them, as I'll be with you for quite some time."

"So I understand."

"All in a good cause. Now then, first item. With your permission, my elves will start with building our quarters. From there they'll construct the factory and ancillary rooms, then shore up and expand the livery stables in order to accommodate the additional caribou. Everything will be connected so it'll be possible to get to and from any of them without having to go outside. This will be convenient during the numerous periods of inclement weather up here."

"That all sounds good, Graham. You'll serve as their supervisor, I assume?"

"If you please. Whatever you say goes, of course. However I was appointed to take charge at the outset due to my extensive experience."

"You have experience in this type of endeavor?"

"No one does. But I do have it in projects that are, in some respects, similar. Or at least vaguely so." He made a mark in his notebook. "Next would be uniforms. What would you like us to wear, sir?"

"I hadn't thought much about that. Whatever they're comfortable working in is good with me, Graham."

"With all due respect Kris Kringle, we are uniting to work for a common goal and we need to look the part. Also, we will be projecting an image to the world, and that being what it is we can't have everyone setting their own styles. It may also help to keep in mind that this is neither a republic nor a democracy. You run the whole show."

"That doesn't seem fair. You're all coming here to live and work- and with no compensation."

Graham held up a hand and waved away Kris's apprehension as if it was an annoying fly. "Please, Kris Kringle. Understand that we were given a choice, and we've made it. No one is here who didn't volunteer and isn't fully aware of the job requirements. Besides, we are compensated. Is not doing something solely for the benefit of mankind a form of payment? Truthfully I happen to think of it as the best kind."

"That is an amazing attitude. And the others think as you do?"

"Yes. And don't sell yourself short either. You would not be in the position you now find yourself in, if someone smarter than both of us did not believe you deserved to be."

"You have a way with words, Graham."

"It has been said. So, about those uniforms?"

This was in no way Kris's area of expertise. "Cathy," he asked. "Any ideas?"

"Well Nicky, I'd think you'd want something unique and fun that would appeal to the young. How about an extra-long shirt, with extended fitted britches tucked into boots that curl up in the front? Oh, and peaked caps with narrow brims to accentuate their pointed ears. Maybe all in a festive red and green color scheme." Graham was writing notes as she spoke.

"Fine with me, honey. Graham?" The elf put down his charcoal writing stick.

"That ensemble will be sufficient. To be honest, anything would be better than this ridiculous suit. I did want to make an impression respectful to your customs upon my arrival, but I've no idea why you humans feel the need to dress so elaborately." His hosts grinned, and he continued. "Mrs. Kringle, some of my elves specialize in tailoring. Would you have any objection to meeting with them as they design the initial outfits; perhaps offer your opinions?"

"I'd be delighted, Graham."

"Thank you. Now then Kris Kringle, later today we'll set up a large canvas tent on-site to serve as our temporary quarters until the permanent structures are built. Have no concerns please, as it will be adequate to our needs. Once the architectural elves arrive this afternoon, they'll go over with you the blueprints for all of the structures that you and I have just discussed. Working under the presumption that you'd agree to this project and, in the interest of saving time, several of them have familiarized themselves with the existing homestead and designed the modification plans in advance. Of course, after viewing them you may request any changes or special accoutrements. In addition, they will also work with you on the custom design and construction of your sleigh. Five will be built in total. Three shall be used in various practice sessions for both you and the reindeer, and one will be stored as a backup. The last is to be employed solely for your Christmas Evening flights."

"It sounds like today will be a busy day," Kris said before taking a sip of tea.

"It shall be." The old sprite then went silent for a moment as he flipped over another page in his notebook. "All right. These last items for the moment regard you specifically, Kris Kringle. First, you too will need a new look. At least for flights and promotional purposes." Graham glanced up momentarily to take notice of his new boss's current, humble attire. "I'm not certain an old linen work shirt and worn trousers is quite in line with the jovial, benevolent look we're going for."

"Was that a joke, Graham?"

"Yes. I am capable of adapting to my surroundings, Kris Kringle," he answered, intentionally without so much as a grin or hint of humor in his voice. At the other end of the kitchen table Cathy smiled again. Rather than annoying, the elder elf's straightforward disposition came across to her as charismatic.

"Now ma'am, would I be correct in assuming that you would also wish to participate in designing your husband's new costume, for lack of a better word?"

"Certainly."

"Brilliant. At present we shall now address perhaps the most important modification of all, Kris Kringle."

"And that is?"

"Your new name."

"Excuse me?"

Graham placed down his notebook and pencil and looked earnestly at the robust native New Englander sitting in front of him. "Sir, you are a human being. You possess a human identity and a human past. And though it's true that you and your wife have been reclusive for quite some time, the names *Kris Kringle* and *Cathy Flake Kringle* are known to others. Whilst you'll remain human, henceforth you will be taking on a completely mythical persona and projecting that persona out to the entire world. This means that you cannot maintain any connection whatsoever to your former identity, at least to those outside of this compound. I hope to make myself very clear on this point sir, as it is of the utmost importance. I'll now respectfully ask that you confirm for me that you fully understand the gravity of what I've just told you."

Graham's words struck home with Kris in a manner he didn't expect. For the first time since Greg Blitzen arrived the day before, the full and entire weight of the mantle of responsibility he'd assumed finally settled in with him. He realized just what he had agreed to sacrifice for the greater good and, further, he knew that there was no longer any way of opting out. But he was also aware that even if there was, he wouldn't take it. That was neither who he was, nor who he would-or even could-ever be. He was a man of his word, to whom integrity above all else stood.

Just then, the Kringle's ancient house cat Comet jumped up on the table to join them; breaking his concentration. Years' worth of furniture scratches were the testament to this beloved family member's presence. And as she had many times previously, Cathy retrieved and gently placed him on the floor. Kris watched with disinterest as he tried to get his thoughts back and couldn't. It didn't really matter, of course. He knew what Graham had said was the reality of the situation. It made perfect sense and was now merely another part of his destiny.

The previous cheeriness in his voice had returned, and he answered the elf with two simple words. "I understand."

"Brilliant," Graham repeated. "And what shall you be wanting to call yourself?"

"Don't you have a name chosen for me?"

"I'm afraid not. You're still an individual, and it's you who'll forever be known by this moniker. So it's yours to create. My suggestion would be to choose something short and snappy."

"My goodness, I don't know."

"Sometimes it's better not to think too long about these things, Kris Kringle."

"You want an answer right now?"

"Can you think of a better time?"

"No, I guess not." Kris thought about it. He gazed around the room looking for some sort of inspiration. In doing so, his eyes met Cathy's.

"Don't look at me, Nicky," she chuckled. "This one's all yours."

"So it is." He continued to look around until he noticed Comet's numerous scratch marks on the kitchen table.

"Claws," he said aloud.

"Excuse me?" Cathy asked.

"Comet's claws. Maybe it's time to trim them. He's an indoor cat, anyway."

"You're stalling, Mr. Kringle," his wife responded merrily.

"Wait a moment here," Graham chimed in. "That's not bad. It's quick and it's easy."

"What is? Comet?" Kris asked.

"Claws."

"You want me to name myself after my cat's talons?"

"Well we can modify the spelling to something more intriguing, of course. Make it seem more mysterious."

"I don't know. It just seems like it's not enough; like there should be more to it than that. Something as big as what we're trying for should have a more prominent name attached, wouldn't you say?"

"Would you agree that the world is a fairly big and complex place, Kris Kringle?"

"Yes of course."

"Yet you humans are quite content to simply call it *Earth*. You see, there really is no need to make things more complicated than necessary."

Kris was astounded at both the wisdom and simplicity of Graham's point. And also that he'd been able to make it with such ease.

"I can see why Greg sent you, my friend. You clearly carry a lot of intellect around in that slight frame."

"You don't generally make it to four-hundred with little more than space between your ears, Kris Kringle. So, will that name be it then?"

"While I see and agree with your logic, I still think there should be more to it." Kris went on to explain why he thought so. "'Most objects, such as *Earth*, go by one name. People, however, almost always have two. *Claws* can be a surname, sure. But another needs to precede it. Something easy and catchy, yet unique."

"Touché, Kris Kringle. Your argument has validity to it."

"Thank you. You don't generally make it to forty-four with…"

he began with a laugh.

"...little more than space between your ears," Graham finished for him with a sigh. "More jokes."

"A little levity is a good thing, my friend."

"You would know better than I. However I shall continue to heed your advice on that subject. Now returning to the matter at hand, what is this preceding name to be?"

"Ah yes, back to business."

Before Kris could say more, Cathy spoke up. "Nicky's always been like a saint to me and our family, Graham. How about that?"

"Saint Claws?" Graham said more as a question to himself rather than a statement to her.

"That's very sweet, Catherine." Kris said. "But don't you think that sounds *just* a little arrogant?"

"Okay. Then how about some version of *Saint* that, combined with *Claws* won't really have any meaning, but will still be appealing? Maybe like *Sante, Santo, Santa...*"

"Just a moment please, Mrs. Kringle," interrupted Graham. "You may be on to something." He paused in thought for a moment while tapping his charcoal stick against the notebook. Then he quickly picked it up and jotted a few words down. "Yes, that looks good." Once finished he looked up at them both. "I think that sounds just right. What do you think?"

"*Santo Claws*?"

"No. *Santa.*"

"Santa Claws?"

"Not quite. Here, look at this." He held up his notebook and turned it around so that they both could see. Cathy leaned in, while Kris could view it from where he was. What they saw written was:

Santi Clawse

Sante Klawse

Santa Claus

Santo Klawhs

"It appears that you like the sound of *Santa Claus*," Kris finally said.

"Not just its sound, Kris Kringle. The aesthetics work too. Wouldn't you agree?"

"I suppose they do at that. *Santa Claus*..." he repeated in order to hear it aloud once more. "Yes, it does have a certain ring to it."

"So, does that settle it then?"

"Cathy?" Kris's inflection turned her name into a one-word question.

"It sounds great to me, Nicky."

"Then that's good enough for me. Yes, Graham. That does indeed settle it. *Santa Claus* it is. Though you can still call me *Kris*."

"Brilliant. And that concludes this morning's business, Kris Kringle. As we still have a few hours until the other elves join us, if you'd like I'll satisfy your curiosity on the background of my people. But first, Mrs. Kringle, have you any biscuits or cookies? I'm famished."

"Why of course, Graham."

"They're fantastic. Why, my Catherine makes the best desserts in the entire Arctic Circle!"

"An incredible feat to be sure considering all the competition," retorted the elf dryly.

The sarcasm from his new subordinate was not lost on Kris. "You really are developing that sense of humor quickly Graham, ho ho ho."

5

Early that afternoon, the rest of the elves arrived and were introduced individually to the Kringle's, William and Charlie. Afterward they split into three groups. The largest went right to work putting up a huge canvas tent adjacent to the main house, as close as possible to where the new construction would take place. As Graham had said, it would serve as the elves temporary quarters while the permanent additions to the homestead were built.

The second group got started on the hours-long process of preparing a massive banquet, as that evening they would all break bread and get to know one another. Most of the elves had been given this new assignment from other projects, and with few exceptions had not met prior to traveling together up to Snowhenge.

The third and by far the smallest group was the Architectural Elves. They presented Kris and Cathy with the previously completed design plans. The first was for the main factory, gift-wrapping and storage areas. Weaving their way past various desks, work and painting stations would be a series of narrow, pulley-operated conveyer belts. Helper Elves would place the unassembled toys on the belts, which would then move them along to their correct destinations based on type and skillset required for completion. After a toy was put together by the Assembly Elves, a separate conveyer would then deliver it to the Wrapping Room, where the Decorative Elves would neatly box and gift-wrap it. Then it would be brought to the Storage Room where the Distribution Elves would stack them carefully based on weight and fragility. These latter elves would also be responsible for taking a quarterly inventory and packing Kris's sleigh between December 18th and 23rd with each year's total inventory.

The mess hall would be located behind the factory. It would serve six full buffet meals daily, one every four hours, and would remain open around the clock. This would ensure that elves on all shifts would be properly fed. Built first would be a group of apartments. Once the entire project was completed the elves' quarters would be attached to the mess hall (and by extension to the main factory), by a heated, above-ground, fully-enclosed connecting passageway. Each elf would have his own furnished room, with size determined by seniority.

Within the week Kris, with considerable input from Graham, would begin giving the elves their assignments based on need and their various areas of expertise. Along with Architectural and Chef Elves he would need to sort out designers, painters, wrappers, plumbers, reindeer trainers, general service, maintenance and foragers. The latter would be split into smaller groups and be continuously out on the road gathering food, wood and supplies. Until the compound was completed, however, nearly all would be either Forager or Carpenter Elves. So they could get started right away when the time came, a few elves would begin designing the toys to be built later. The architects would appoint a small number of foremen to oversee the compound construction work and make certain it was done correctly.

Once the operation was up and running smoothly, any elf would be able to talk with Kris Kringle directly. For the most part though, Graham would serve as Kris's liaison to them. As well as his second-in-command.

When the discussion was over the architects excused

themselves and left the room. After they'd gone, Cathy sat down next to her husband and patted his hand with her usual warmth.

"Well Nicky, it seems that our new life has truly begun."

"Yes, dear. I just hope I'm up to the challenge."

"Kristopher, there is no one in the world who is more so." She smiled the angelic smile that Kris had fallen in love with from the very first day that they had met. He mirrored it with one of his own, while silently hoping that she was right.

6

The Meet-and-Greet dinner that night was a huge success. Afterward a bonfire was built on the huge expanse of snow-covered earth that served as Kris and Cathy's front yard. As the Kringle's hoped, the many elves who hadn't yet had a chance to get acquainted took this opportunity to do so. The few who had worked together before were able to reacquaint themselves. The Kringle's walked around and mingled with everyone. William and Charlie opened the livery doors so that reindeer both old and new could join the frivolity. The elves who'd had previous animal training took to them right off.

Nutmeg ambled over toward his old master, and Kris's eyes lit up when he saw him.

"Nutty, ol' buddy!" Kris said in cheerful greeting while draping an arm around his old companion's bridle. "How are you this fine evening, my friend?"

He could tell something was saddening his most-valued reindeer merely by the look on his face. And he'd had an idea of what it was.

"Listen," Kris said softly as he and the sullen caribou turned away from the others. "I know it probably seems a little overwhelming to suddenly be sharing your home with so many other reindeer, but you'll never get lost in the shuffle. We go way back. We're family, you and I, and nothing will ever change that. I also need you now more than ever, as your experience and leadership will be a great help to me with the others. Can I count on you, Nutmeg?"

The reindeer managed a smile and, happier than he'd been before, nuzzled his head against Kris's arm in typical reindeer fashion to show him that yes, he could very well count on him. Kris smiled and looked him straight in the eyes. "I thank you, old friend."

7

The next day, construction of the new facilities at Snowhenge began. The elves worked at a furious pace as the days passed. As January turned into February, and then into March, land was cleared, basements dug, and foundations poured. As a result the exteriors of the new structures had begun to take shape. The same wind-resistant torches used at the inaugural banquet had been repositioned all around the burgeoning compound. They were required to be continually lit and maintained due to the exceptionally short amount of sunlight the area received in winter. The elves also had dozens of portable oil lamps that were continually moved around, based on specific interior or underground lighting needs.

As the year went further into springtime and beyond, the days began to grow a little longer and the temperatures more bearable. Six days a week, on a specially-landscaped tract of land nestled within a natural hollow three-hundred yards from the homestead, a dozen elves trained thirty-two reindeer. They were split into four teams of eight. Six elves worked with two groups from Monday through Wednesday, and the other six worked with the remaining two Thursday through Saturday. In late November all of their hard work would culminate in a Reindeer Olympics, or *Deerlympics*;

named after the Games held in ancient Greece. All caribou would be graded on several categories, and the best eight would then be placed together to form Santa Claus's Christmas Eve sleigh team.

On July 9th Kris Kringle walked over to that area, which had been dubbed *Cathy's Glen*. He watched as two of the reindeer ran side-by-side at full stride across a narrow, angled, snow-covered wooden platform before coming to a full stop. The design was meant to mimic an actual rooftop so the caribou could practice in an environment as close to the real one as possible. The reindeer on the left side skidded slightly, while his mate on the right stopped on a dime. An instructor stood nearby watching them, then making notes on a chart. Kris looked around until he spotted the lead coach and called over to him.

"Basil, join me for a moment please." The elf went over to him straightaway.

"Good morning, Mr. Kringle."

"Good morning. I'm just checking up on the teams. I know there's still a while yet to go, but are there any new standouts?"

"Well the four whose ability you'd noticed right off and named yourself last winter are still among the top five performers: Donner, Cupid, Blitzen and Comet. Rounding out that group of five is Carlisle, who has come along splendidly."

"Good. Have any others managed to close the gap much?"

"Sir there are," Basil consulted his paper, "six others who have really begun to show their true potential."

"And they are?"

"Ah, let's see," he glanced down to his paper once more. "Dancer, Vixen, Linus, Noel, Prancer and Dasher."

"All grading well, you say?"

"All *A's* apiece over their past eight sessions."

"Excellent, Basil. Thank you. I'll leave you to your drills."

"Anytime. I'm happy to help, sir."

With their exchange completed, Kris Kringle headed back toward the factory. Just as he had when he'd ambled out to the Glen, he noticed the walk taking a little more out of him than it had in the past. While never a small man, he seemed to have put on some extra weight over the past few months.

Twenty minutes after they'd finished dinner that night Kris was in his parlor standing over a large table. He was looking down upon the three-foot long solid pine board that was lying across it. On the far top end of either side he had already bored through identical holes, each one half-inch in diameter. Carved into the middle-left side were the letters *NOR*. He was leaning over to begin carving a *T* when Cathy came in.

"It's looks wonderful, Nicky."

"You think so? Good. Tonight I'll finish the *NORTH POLE* lettering, and ask Graham to have an elf affix it to a post in our yard after the ceremonies tomorrow."

"It's all really starting to come along, isn't it dear?"

Kris put his carving tool down and accepted the cup of tea Cathy was holding out to him. "Yes love, it is. Everything relevant is now complete," then he added with a bit of pride, and ahead of schedule. The grand opening is at 7 a.m. After that the toy making will commence in earnest."

"That's amazing. Is there nothing left to be done?"

"Nothing save the painting and application of festive decorations throughout the compound. But that can easily be accomplished as a side project next January. We've already used up nearly seven months of this year getting everything ready, and those poor elves are going to have to put in a titanic effort to get our inventory up to requirements."

"Can they do it?"

"I think so. I've never seen such a determined lot. Their work ethic is second-to-none of any group I've ever encountered."

"Maybe we should do something for them to show our appreciation."

"I've already thought of that, Cathy. Next winter, after the aesthetic work on the compound is complete we'll build a multi-use recreational area for them to enjoy in their off-hours. To start, it'll contain a restaurant, piano, comfortable furniture, billiard tables and a rather impressive library."

"That's a fantastic idea, Nicky!" she beamed.

"As you've said, they've earned it." Kris took a swig of his tea.

"Well then, I shall leave you to your carving. Don't keep at it too late."

"No, I won't. I'll be along soon." As she left he looked back to the pine, and paused briefly to think upon all that tomorrow meant for everyone at Snowhenge. After a moment's consideration, he went back to work on his sign.

8

At exactly 6:59 a.m. July 10th, 1821, Kris and Cathy Kringle stepped over the threshold that separated their main house from the new factory. What they saw as they did made Kris smile, and had Cathy fighting back tears. All three-hundred elves, fully outfitted in their new red and green apparel, were standing at attention at their individual work stations. Twenty feet in front of the Kringle's, strung from one wall completely across the plant from the other, was a large ice-blue colored ribbon. On a table off to the left rested a huge, four-tiered candy cane-embedded cake, with green and red frosting surrounding the entire bottom layer.

"Ho-ho-ho," Kris bellowed. "And haven't you all outdone yourselves?!"

Graham stepped forward with two wooden boxes in either hand. He extended the one in his right to Kris. "Go ahead, Kris Kringle. Open it, please."

Without another word Kris did so and saw that the box contained a large pair of scissors. He smiled.

"Elves, please do gather 'round," he spoke out in an elevated voice so that all may hear him with ease. "Your amazing work under adverse weather and lighting conditions this past year has been nothing short of extraordinary. And in truth it's about to get even tougher. But I will be rewarding your efforts. I'll also remind you that while in the coming years there may be occasional difficulties, none should equal those we've faced getting ready for this first Christmas season. You see we are pioneers, and like all pioneers we possess an instinct both to lead and to accomplish great things. And now we -you all, really- have done just that with this spectacular achievement." To punctuate his words he swept his free hand in an arc to indicate that he'd meant the entire building.

It was Graham who spoke next. "It was our pleasure. We thank you for being the kind of boss whom his employees wish to impress." Before Kris could answer, the old sprite continued. "Now, before you cut this ribbon Kris Kringle, the time has come to make an official clarification." He turned sideways so that he could address both the Kringle's and the elves. "From this day forward, to me, to my colleagues, and to the world, you will no longer be known as "Kris Kringle." Henceforth and in perpetuity, you are "Santa Claus," and will be referred to as such. Except of course by me in private." Laughter greeted Graham's ad-libbed, though honest, addendum. "With that said…ladies and gentlemen, please allow me to introduce to you Mr. and Mrs. Santa Claus!" The room erupted in applause as Graham and Kris shook hands. "And now, Santa, would you please do the honors?"

"Gladly." Kris stepped up to the ribbon, opened the scissors, and in one deft move sliced it cleanly in half. As both sides fell to the floor another round of applause was made. When it died down Graham handed Kris the second box. He opened it to find a rather amusingly large key in the shape of a candy cane.

"Everyone, I'd like to officially welcome you to Santa's Workshop. And as soon as Mr. Claus turns that key, we'll be open for business!" Even more clapping ensued, and at its end Santa spoke. "I owe so much of who I am to the woman standing to my left, and I rarely get the chance to showcase just how much she means to me. What I'm saying Cathy, is since you already own the key to my heart, please also take the key to my Workshop. Let's start it up together!"

Cathy blushed hard and hugged her husband tightly. While doing so, and in a voice low enough so that only they could hear, she whispered "I'm so proud of you, Nicky." She took the key and stepped toward the oversized key box that it was obviously meant for. Cathy stuck the key in and pushed it forward until she heard it click into place. Then, after taking a moment to look up at everyone, turned it clockwise ninety degrees. Within seconds, the whirring sounds of moving conveyer belts became audible as a very rudimentary set of white overhead lights slowly began to brighten. These last caught Santa Claus by complete surprise, and he took Graham aside. "Are those powered with what I think they're powered with?"

"Electricity, yes. It's running the pulley system, too." Graham answered happily. "Of course, it's still a very crude set-up, but it will prove to be much more effective than running the workshop manually. Also we shall be continually upgrading, as improvements in that technology will certainly be forthcoming."

Kris Kringle remained stunned. "But nobody's been able to harness electricity in such a capacity."

"Well, Santa Claus, what can I tell you? We're not "nobody." You can expect more from us. Now, sir, unless I'm mistaken you have a cake to cut." Graham grinned at him brightly.

"Ho-ho-ho," Kris laughed while holding his still expanding stomach. "My friend, you've never failed to astound." Santa Claus then turned back and went toward both the cake and the crowd that awaited him.

After lunch that day Kris returned to the workshop carrying his completed *NORTH POLE* sign to see how things were going. Though it was impossible for him to go unnoticed, he tried to remain as nondescript as he could. He was dressed in his normal attire of a white long-sleeved linen work shirt and dark blue trousers. There had been one recent, slight alteration to his wardrobe, however. Cathy had let the trousers out at the waist to allow for his weight gain. For additional comfort, he had also begun to wear suspenders.

Kris walked across the factory floor and marveled at how well everyone seemed to already be working in unison. At the start of one conveyer belt a group of elves would repeatedly place similar small stacks of wood, screws, and any other materials that a given toy required; one after another. As the belt made its way through the individual workstations of each Engineer Elf, he would take the stack, place it on his desk, and use whatever specific tools were needed to assemble it right there.

Once work on the toy was completed, he would simply turn and place it back on the belt where it would travel to the workstations of the Painting and Designing Elves. Kris watched as one member of this group took an assembled boat off the conveyer. He added on little canvas sails and a working miniature ship's wheel. The latter came complete with multiple spokes which a real helmsman would use to steer his vessel through difficult seas. Once it had been secured, he gave it a quick spin 'round to make sure it wasn't affixed too tightly, and therefore wouldn't stick. Satisfied after observing it make one complete turn, he began the process of painting it from top to bottom. When finished with his impeccable work, he placed the toy on a separate conveyer belt that slowly circled the entire factory before disappearing through a hole in the wall that led into the packaging area. This conveyer was by far - and intentionally- the workshop's most leisurely moving belt. Its extra-long trip allowed any paint on a given toy to dry, and any glue to set.

Kris noted that the entire process, from removing it from the first conveyer and placing it upon the second, took no more than four minutes. That was extraordinary work. And teamwork too, once he included how quickly the initial elf had put the boat together.

Kris walked toward the separated back rooms, and along the way stopped off at Graham's station to give him the North Pole sign. The elf was away, so he took a charcoal stick from on top of the desk and wrote a quick note asking for it to be installed outside, when convenient. He then carried on to the Packaging Room. Inside there were two tables, thirty-feet apiece in length; each with ten elves sitting at them.

Two burly elves, as oxymoronic as such a description sounds, tended the conveyer. As the toys came by they removed them in turn, walked to the table and placed them in front of whichever elf did not currently have a gift before him to work on.

All of the wrappers had their own scissors, tape, tags, glue and rulers. Behind the chairs upon which they sat were a countless number of boxes, ribbons, bows and tissue paper in a variety of colors and all within easy reach. As each toy was brought to them, they would carefully package it, wrap it, label it, and attach the appropriate ornamental trimmings. Then they'd set it on the far right-hand corner of their workspaces. Shortly thereafter, either of another pair of workers would retrieve it and load it onto one of two pallets, with each sitting upon a dolly. One pallet was for the sturdy gifts; the other, for the fragile.

Once a pallet was full an elf would push its dolly through the large doors and into the enormous adjoining Storage Room. When it was emptied they'd push the dolly back into the Wrapping Room, reload it, and start all over again.

For about twenty minutes Kris watched the process in action. As in the main workshop it was seamless. Greg Blitzen had most assuredly assigned to him the best of the best of elves. Once again very pleased with what he saw, he decided to go into the mess hall for a snack and some hot cocoa.

After selecting a sugared doughnut Kris filled up a mug with cocoa and went to find a seat. He chose an empty table near the front, and had only just sat down when he heard a voice chime out from behind him.

"Mind if I join you, Santa?" It was Basil, the lead reindeer trainer.

"Why, not at all, Basil. Please do."

"Thank you, sir." The elf took a seat next to the much larger man and placed his own mug of cocoa on the table.

"Is this a social visit, or do you have some news to relate?"

"Sir, I just thought you might like to hear how things are going in the Glen."

"By all means, Basil. Please proceed."

"Thank you. Now as you're aware your Christmas Eve team won't be finalized until after the November *Deerlympics*. However we still need to assemble our best current performers before then so that you can start practicing your own trial runs."

"Yes, I'm aware of that." Kris had known that sooner or later he himself would have to get accustomed to driving a flying sleigh pulled by a team of reindeer. Even after all he'd been through, and even though he knew that it was completely feasible, the concept still nevertheless seemed ludicrous. The simple fact was that he wasn't at all looking forward to 'Sleigh-driving practice,' if that's what one even called such a thing.

"Well Santa, we've scheduled your first practice flights for August. In advance of that, as I've mentioned, we've been working to put that first-string team together."

"August? That's next month, Basil."

"Yes, sir. I know. But there's a lot of ground to cover, both literally and figuratively. It's not just about flying the team, it's about taking them up and landing them properly. And by *them* I mean you too, sir. Frankly, you'll be traveling at inconceivable speeds in an open-air transport vehicle, whilst performing countless starts and stops in every possible weather condition imaginable. There's also Chimney Avoidance training. And let's just thank goodness that we don't yet have to worry about the countless assortment of inconveniently placed TV antennas."

"TV antennas?"

Basil held up his hand. "Never mind, sir. It's a story for another century."

"I see."

"At any rate, here's the preliminary practice team as it stands now: Blitzen, Donner, Carlisle, Cupid, Noel, Comet, Dancer, and Prancer."

"And they're the best?"

"Yes, but once again it's very close. Dasher, Linus, and Vixen have also performed extremely well in our preliminary reindeer games."

"All right, Basil. I'll trust in your judgment."

"Thank you, Santa. So you'll know for your calendar, your first official run-through with the caribou will be August 21st at 8 a.m."

"I'll remember," came the reply in an uncharacteristically melancholic tone.

For a few minutes after they both sat in silence drinking their cocoas. Finally Basil spoke. "So, Santa. Seen any good movies lately?"

"What do you mean?" he said while gazing off distantly, not really looking at anything.

"Just a joke, sir. Trying to break the monotony is all."

"Another story for another century, I take it."

"Well, technically speaking, not quite."

"Later this one, then?"

"Yes."

"Basil?"

"Yes, sir?"

"I'm going to sit here and finish my cocoa now."

"Right, sir." But the elf missed the rather obvious hint and, instead of leaving, simply stared ahead quietly and finished his cocoa, too.

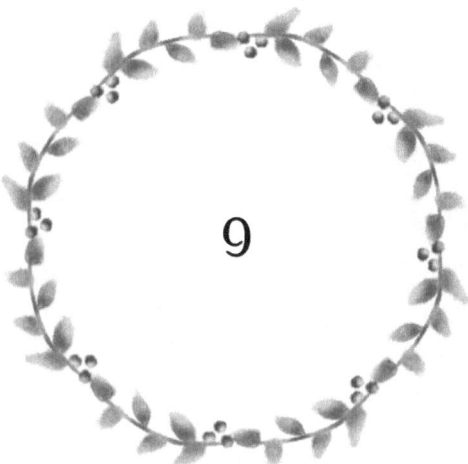

9

As the days continued to move along, the workshop's inventory grew at a tremendous rate. Kris even hand-carved two separate wooden models for the elves to recreate: a boat and a log cabin.

Eventually August 21st arrived and on that morning Kris found himself seated in the largest, most elegantly designed sleigh he'd ever seen. The exterior was painted a deep forest green with red trim, and all sides were emblazed with a perfect, hand-stenciled reproduction of his signature. Draped over the front of his sleigh were the reins attached to his eight-reindeer team. He was dressed in his green parka with a wool cap pulled down tightly over his head, and had very little idea of what he was supposed to do. A pair of elves were holding the two lead reindeer, which kept the entire team stationary.

Basil walked over to the port side of the sleigh.

"Okay, Santa. Let's get this first practice-run underway. Remember, they know what to do. Your responsibility is to get the sleigh in the air, guide them, and then land. This initial try is fairly straightforward. It'll be an easy, five-hundred yard flight. In fact if you squint you can make out the flags at the finish line."

"Not even with my spectacles."

"Oh, right. That reminds me. Here." Basil handed his boss a pair of goggles.
"What am I supposed to do with these?"

"Santa, these goggles are fitted with crystal-clear, fog-free lenses and will fit completely over your spectacles. They'll help greatly in the windy conditions you'll be facing whilst allowing you optimal visibility."

"They look ridiculous, Basil," he said while looking them over.

"Who cares?" He answered a little more flippantly than he'd intended. "No one's going to see you, anyway. The images of you that we'll be sending out into the world will not include them."

"If you say so," Kris answered while pulling them over his head. "All right, let's get this over with."

"As you wish. Elves!" Basil yelled over to the two up front, "We're a go. Please release the deer and back away." They did as they were told. When his path was fully cleared, Kris took up the reins. "Okay, deer. Let's make this ride nice and smooth. All right Comet, Blitzen, Carlisle, Noel, Donner, Cupid, Prancer and Dancer. Ready? Let's go!" He gave the reins a quick shake and the team began to move. They built up speed much quicker than Kris had expected, until it occurred to him that they'd have to be able to manage that with only a few dozen feet of 'runway' per rooftop. They had clearly been well-trained. Shortly the sleigh began to elevate. It leveled off at around fifty feet of altitude where he could already see the flags. Immediately he pulled back on the reins to signal his desire to begin descent, and in an instant they headed back toward the earth. The hooves of the two lead deer, Comet and Carlisle, hit the ground effortlessly and the entire sleigh came to a stop with its back nearly even with the flags on either side of it.

The only glitch, barely noticeable as it was, was that Noel had slid two inches while his seven colleagues had come to an immediate, flawless stop. The slight miscue caused the sleigh to end up almost imperceptibly askew. Kris moved to exit, and immediately the elves stationed at the finish line were already racing over to assist him. By the time he got out Basil had joined them.

"That was fantastic, Santa!" He exclaimed, slightly out of breath. He glanced over to one of the descent elves, who silently turned his clipboard around for basil to throw a quick glance at. "Eight out of ten on your first try!"

"You know, that didn't go near as poorly as I'd expected. Just give me a minute and we'll go again, Basil."

"Yes, sir!"

Over the next four hours they repeatedly practiced multiple maneuvers; stopping only when lunchtime came around. Kris left the sleigh for the final time that day and headed back toward the mess hall while his team was led back to Cathy's Glen for feeding. By the time Kris had settled down to a hearty mid-day repast he was feeling much more confident about how things were going. He decided to set a goal of finishing the drills in half the time at his next practice session in early September.

He took a drink of his cocoa, then promptly put the mug back down after realizing how tired of it he was getting. It seemed like he was having cocoa with every meal now. Though his mood was still cheerful, he went back to the buffet line for a hot cup of tea.

"Alec," Kris said to the Serving Elf standing behind the buffet table. "Would you mind getting me some tea?"

"Sure thing, Santa. No cocoa?"

"I think I've had enough cocoa for a while. Why is there so much of it? In fact there seems to be a lot of meal repetition lately."

"I couldn't tell you, sir, "Alec answered while handing him his tea. "Nigel's the menu department. I'm only Sustenance Distribution."

"Right."

"I do have some fresh apple pie, Santa. We haven't had that in a while. Can I cut you a piece?"

"Sure."

"With ice cream or a slice of cheddar?"

"Cheddar cheese on pie?" Kris asked politely but with barely concealed disinterest.

"Yes, sir. It's popular in Vermont. Aren't you a New Englander?"

"Yes, Connecticut. But that's southern New England. Vermont's in the northern region."

"Oh. Well geography aside, it's rather tasty."

Kris sighed, wondering how he'd gotten into this conversation. "All right, then. Let's try the cheddar."

"Coming up."

As he returned to finish his half-eaten meal he found Graham sitting across from him.

"Ah, Graham. How're things in the workshop?" He queried while reaching for the sugar bowl.

"Good, good. And I hear you're doing well with your sleigh trials."

"Word travels fast."

"Sure it does. The Glen's only three hundred yards away, and as your Chief-of-Staff all departments keep me in the loop."

"I guess they would at that," Kris said while stirring a teaspoon of sugar into his beverage. Then he broke off a bit of the pie and cheese before pitching a forkful into his mouth.

"That cheddar? Those Foraging Elves do earn their keep. Vermont's thousands of miles east."

Kris dropped the now-empty fork on his plate. "Is there anything you guys don't know?"

"I've seen my share, Kris Kringle. I'm a four-hundred year-old world traveler."

"You all are, I think. Incidentally that reminds me; it seems that you're all British. Not that that that in itself matters at all, of course. It's just that I've learned that nothing regarding this project is due to coincidence. I'd just thought elves existed everywhere, so it'd seem like at least one of you would be from America. Or somewhere else."

"America hasn't yet existed long enough to produce much of an elf population, and I think Greg Blitzen's goal was to assemble an entire crew who can speak fluent English. That way any of us could easily communicate with you."

"I would think all elves would be capable of speaking in every language."

"Why?" Graham retorted. "We're not genies in bottles. Sure we have many extraordinary talents, but we can't do everything. If that was the case we wouldn't be subordinate to anyone. We'd be running the whole show instead of you."

"That's a fair point."

"I'm glad you think so."

"Indeed."

Kris went back to his pie and cheddar while Graham drank from his mug of cocoa.

"So," Kris asked. "Everything go well at the factory this morning?"

"Quite well, thank you."

"Good."

"And how's Mrs. Claus?"

"She's excellent. Thank you for asking."

"Not at all."

There was an awkward minute of silence between them.

"Graham is there anything you'd like to report; anything you need?"

"No."

"Okay. Well, is there any reason why we're just sitting here not really talking about anything?"

"Filler, sir."

"Filler?"

"Yes. The author thinks it might be wise to stretch this novella out occasionally, either with arguably witty repartee, or meaningless dialogue that pays off when we break the Fourth Wall for comic relief. That's not often done in literature, so why not give it a go? The thing is, an entire year has to be covered in a relatively short amount of pages, Kris Kringle. And while this book is certainly a fresh, interesting take on your myth, once described, a lot of what we do up here can become redundant to hear. And let's face it, attention spans are not what they used to be. Or at least what they will be after they gradually decrease from another century and a half of this relative status quo."

"Fascinating. I never thought of it that way, Graham. So now that we've 'stretched this chapter out' as far as it can likely go, what's next?"

"I suppose we could revisit that coal debate."

Kris sighed. "No, not again. I've told you it's ridiculous. Not receiving a Christmas gift for poor behavior is sufficient. There's no need to be tossing coal into stockings to augment the disappointment. Besides, we have no room in which to store it. And I'm not pulling essential foragers off of their important task to send them off to go coal mining."

"All right, all right," Graham answered. "You asked."

"Yes, that's true. So what do we do now, then?"

"I guess we could just move along to Chapter 10."

"Okay. And thanks for the earlier clarifying exposition."

"Anytime, Kris Kringle. It's what I'm here for. Or evidently in this chapter, at least."

10

As the weeks wore on summer melted into autumn as the short, cold northern Alaskan days once again grew even shorter and colder still. Amazingly, by October the Storage Room was over 80% full. Now into November the *Deerlympics* had arrived and would serve as the final determining factor for which a lucky few caribou would earn the opportunity to forever become a part of history.

Several of the elves who were not working shifts came by to watch. Some stood just behind the marked sidelines, and some brought blankets to lay over the packed snow. Most of the latter group also had small picnic lunches. Nutmeg, who was too old to participate, still came out to support his fellow caribou. Kris stood next to Basil on the interior part of the course so he could communicate directly with the trainers throughout. In the *Deerlympics*, they were to be graded and evaluated on takeoffs, landings, speed of elevation, descent and overall stamina.

All thirty-two deer had performed excellently over the course of their training. As such, it had been difficult for any to unseat the eight who had initially won the job of driving Santa Claus's sleigh during his rehearsal drills. The events were intense, and all throughout the day a light snow fell over reindeer, trainers and spectators alike.

When the Games had at last concluded, Basil conferred with Kris Kringle and his assistants for a brief, three-minute conversation. Then he called the top ten performers over to them. They were: Carlisle, Cupid, Comet, Blitzen, Noel, Vixen, Donner, Prancer, Dancer and Dasher.

"Reindeer," Basil said loudly, "you have all performed admirably, and have every reason to be proud of yourselves and each other. You are the ten best flying reindeer in the world, and eight of you are going to drive Santa Claus's inaugural flight. I'll now call out the names of those eight. However before I do; to the two who didn't make this cut you have absolutely nothing to be ashamed of. Your efforts have been outstanding, and you shall be the first alternates in the event that a substitute is needed. The sleigh's maximum requirement of an eight-reindeer team is the sole reason why two of you are being cut today." Basil then lifted his clipboard up so he could read it and, as he did, noticed Carlisle shaking his head to try and get his attention.

"Carlisle?"

Carlisle walked over to both Santa and the head trainer. As he did, both immediately noticed a limp in his gait. "Gareth," Basil shouted out to his head Veterinarian Elf. "Come quickly!"

Gareth was there in seconds. He saw Carlisle's front left leg extended and without a word began tending to it. As he did so everyone went quiet. Basil and Claus exchanged concerned glances. Five minutes later Gareth stood up and addressed them both. "The good news gentlemen is that nothing is broken. He'll be all right, but he does have a severe muscle sprain and a possible tear that…"

"…will take weeks if not months to properly heal," Kris finished for him.

Gareth looked up at his boss. "That sir is, in fact, the bad news."

Kris looked over to the sidelines and caught the eyes of both William and Charlie. He signaled for them to come over, and then for Basil and Gareth to step back. He then went to Carlisle and put an arm around him. Leaning in toward the side of his head and with a greatly-lowered voice, he told him: "Carlisle, the pain you had to endure just to finish these events must have been unbearable. Yet not once did you ever complain or even acknowledge your injury to anyone. You have made me tremendously proud, and have my deepest gratitude for your determination and professionalism. Further, I think you should know that you had made my team. In fact you had not only earned your spot, but came in ranked first overall. Now I don't know whether telling you that helps things or makes them worse, but I chose to mention it because, if it were me, I'd want to know."

Carlisle leaned his head into Santa's shoulder and made an up and down motion with it to re-assure him that he'd made the right decision; he had wanted to know.

It was then that Charlie and William reached them. Kris quickly gave both his instructions. "Billy, Chuck, I'd like you to escort Carlisle back to the livery stable and assist Gareth with anything he needs. Gareth, unless otherwise notified he is to be your first priority. Am I clear?" All three of them answered "Yes, sir", in unison. Kris patted Carlisle gently on the back. And as he was being led away he turned his head back toward him and nodded it up and down one more time. Kris smiled at him. As they walked off every elf in attendance gave Carlisle a hearty round of applause. It continued unabated until the party of four reached the stable.

With Carlisle off receiving medical attention, the business at hand continued. Once again Basil and Kris stood side-by-side, which accentuated the absurd difference in height between the quite diminutive elf and his 6'3" human boss.

"With Carlisle now out, how this will work is that the ninth-highest scoring reindeer will automatically take his vacated spot. Vixen, that's you." The faint sound of clapping could be heard from the sidelines. "That leaves one place left, and for it we will have a change in the lineup. Noel, your performance this year has been nothing short of exemplary, and as stated I have nothing but the highest regard and praise for your efforts. Nevertheless, you will not be on the final squad this year; you'll be the first alternate. Thank you for your efforts, Noel. Now, based on his incredible showing today and resolute persistence all throughout training, Dasher has earned the last position on Santa's Sleigh Team. Exceptional job, Dasher." Dasher nodded at Basil while Noel, with his head justifiably held high, left to join the other caribou who were watching the proceedings.

With the Final Eight reindeer together at last, Basil turned toward his superior. The snow was coming down much harder now, but that did not matter one single iota. He looked up into the driving flakes toward the face of Kris Kringle, and announced as loudly as he could for the benefit of those in attendance: "Santa Claus, I am happy, pleased and proud to present to you your inaugural team of reindeer for the year Eighteen-Hundred and Twenty-One. I give you Cupid, Comet, Dancer, Donner, Blitzen, Prancer, Vixen and Dasher!"

Kris stepped forward. "Gentledeer, it will be my great pleasure to fly with all of you next month. Due to your hard work and dedication, the entire world will soon know and revere each of your names. I congratulate every one of you." His new team stomped their right paws down in unison three times in a salute. Santa Claus himself then applauded, and was joined by the trainer and spectator elves.

11

On Thursday November 29, 1821, Santa and Mrs. Claus, Charlie, William and the entire staff of elves took the whole day off to celebrate the Bicentennial of America's original Thanksgiving holiday. It was also a chance to revel together in their near-miraculous achievements over this first year. They had begun and finished the entire North Pole complex in just over six months. And with less than that left in 1821 to create a year's worth of toys, and only a month 'til Christmas, the Storage Room was already almost full with inventory. The reindeer were all fully-trained and Santa Claus had graduated from his sleigh flying course with top marks.

Every one of Santa's elves could legitimately look back on what they'd accomplished with great pride.

Numerous large tables and hundreds of folding chairs had been brought out into the front yard of Kris and Cathy's main residence. The Chef Elves had been in the kitchen all day preparing roast turkey, stuffing, potatoes, sweet potatoes, cranberries, green beans, lobsters, crabmeat, and fresh bread; along with a variety of cheeses. Also pumpkin, apple and mincemeat pies. The feast was part traditional, part modern, and part innovative. Since the elves already knew what would be served at future Thanksgiving dinners, they had requested it be obtained by the foragers over a month in advance. As before, the stable doors were left open so the reindeer, who'd been fed first, could walk around and mingle with the others at Snowhenge.

For two hours everyone ate to his or her fill and then broke away from the tables to socialize. This went on for another few hours before Kris asked if he could have their attention. When they had quieted down Graham handed him a bullhorn. But after hearing the first few words he'd spoken through it and becoming annoyed at the sound, Kris discarded it and simply spoke in a louder voice.

"Good evening, everyone," he began. "I won't take up too much of your time because, more than anyone, I know how much you deserve this day off. I just wanted to sincerely thank you for everything you've managed to achieve this year."

"You're the best, Santa!" An unfamiliar voice shouted from one of the tables.

"That's so very kind, ho-ho-ho." He chuckled in a way that'd become familiar to them all. "But it's easy to be a good boss when everyone who works for you is as competent as all of you!"

His very sincere compliment resulted in more cheering and applause.

When it subsided, Kris continued. "This December we're going to make history. I'm going to need you more than ever from now until then." He paused a moment as if to determine whether he should say more. He decided that yes, he should.

"While I was going to save this bit of news until after Christmas, I've decided to tell you now instead. Although I'll keep its amenities as a surprise, I have already authorized the Architectural Elves to begin in January construction of a large, fully-enclosed rest and recreational area for use and enjoyment of every elf at Snowhenge!"

This generated a symphony of cheers.

"No, no. None of that," Kris interrupted. "Each and every one of you has earned this. And now just one more thing from Cathy and then I'll encourage you to spend the rest of the evening enjoying yourselves with food and friendship. Cathy?" He extended his hand to help his wife up onto to the podium that he was standing on.

"I have very little to add," she shouted. "I just wanted to echo the words of my husband and add two more: Happy Thanksgiving!" More cheers greeted them as both Cathy and Kris re-took their seats. Before anyone went back to celebrating however, Graham stood up and addressed the Clause's. "Just a token of our appreciation, Mr. and Mrs. Claus." He handed them a beautiful custom house address sign made out of solid cherry wood. On it was carved *1225 Christmas Lane*, along with decorative images of holly leaves.

Cathy spoke first, "Oh Graham, this is so lovely. Our thanks to all of you!"

"Please, Mrs. Claus. As Santa said to us, so I will say to you: we'll hear none of that. It's what we do." He finished with a hearty laugh. Instead of protesting, both Clauses joined in on the laughter.

Afterward the eating, revelry and merriment continued well into the night.

12

December had finally arrived.

As the days passed the snowfall intensified, just as had the jitters in Kris's stomach. His first global voyage was quickly approaching, and there was no slowing or stopping the steady march of Time. Late in the evening of December 16th, after trying fruitlessly for hours to get some sleep, Kris got out of bed and threw a robe on over his pajamas. He left the bedroom quietly so as not to awaken Cathy, then went downstairs and made himself tea. When it was ready he walked through the connecting doors while carrying the cup with him into the factory.

After throwing a quick glance toward the overnight shift of engineers and painters who were absorbed in their work, he bypassed them and entered the Storage Room. Looking around, he saw that it was nearly filled to the brim with brightly colored packages. Near the base of Gift Mountain was a singular elf sitting in a simple folding chair. Normally there'd be two, and Kris correctly assumed that his partner was currently in the Wrapping Room loading up another one of the endless pallets. He walked over toward the lone elf, who immediately stood at attention when he saw Santa Claus coming his way.

"Please, Edmund. At ease," Kris ordered gently. Edmund

relaxed and turned toward him.

"Good evening, Santa Claus. How may I be of service to you?"

"I need nothing. I can't sleep, so I thought I'd take a walk." He gazed up one more time at the myriad presents before him and still couldn't help but be astounded by their sheer volume. After a couple of seconds he turned his attention back to the elf.

"How long have you been doing various projects like this, Edmund?"

"This is only my second job, sir," He answered swiftly. "I'm among the youngest of your elves. I just turned 57 in October."

"57?"

"Yes, sir. I'm from Somerset, England. Born in 1764. And you? If you don't mind me asking."

"Connecticut, 1776."

"Ah, well yes. We do take longer to get going than you humans do, I suppose."

"I suppose so." Kris paused a moment and changed the conversation up a bit. "Just over a week and I'll be off with the team, Edmund. Are you sure you and your partner can fit all of those boxes into my little sleigh?"

"Well it won't be just me and him, sir. We'll have help, of course. But yes, well get the job done. You can rest assured, Santa. And if I may be so presumptuous sir, 'tis my belief that this first trip will go off just fine. You've got a great team behind you." He stopped, and right before Kris thought he would say nothing further, Edmund continued. "You see sir, if you should fail then we all will fail. And I can promise you that none of us is going to let that happen. This project is simply too important to not be successful."

Kris smiled at the confident sprite. "Thank you, Edmund. You've been a great help."

"'Tis my pleasure and honour, sir," he said with utmost sincerity.

"Please, have a seat and continue your rest. You're going to need it. We all are."

"As you say, sir." Edmund sat down.

Kris turned and walked back through the workshop toward the main house.

13

On the morning of Christmas Eve, Kris went down to the kitchen and found Cathy already there and in the process of making him breakfast. He went over to her, and with her hands full she could only tilt her cheek toward him. He gave it a quick kiss and asked if he could help.

"Of course not, Kris Kringle. Now please seat yourself as this is ready." He did as he was told. She filled a plate with bacon, cheese and buttermilk biscuits and brought it over to him. Cathy placed it down next to a full butter dish and a large glass of fresh orange juice. "Happy birthday, my love," she said.

"Aww, Cathy. You didn't have to get up so early and do all this."

"Have to" has nothing to do with it, Nicky. I wanted to. Happy 45th, dear."

"Thank you, sweetheart. I'd better eat up anyway as I'll need all the strength I can get for tonight." She smiled and placed a small box beside him. He looked up at her and, without a word, put his utensils down, picked it up and opened it. From the box he took a snowball constructed from the finest silk he'd ever seen.

"This is marvelous, Cathy. Where did you get it?"

"I made it, of course. For our Snowhenge anniversary last January you brought me a snowflake, and so for your birthday I made you an entire snowball. I love you, Nicky."

"Like you Cathy, it's more than I deserve. Thank you with all of my heart for everything you do for me; for everything you mean to me." Before he could go on with the sentiment there was a knock at the front door.

"Stay here and eat, Nicky, I'll get it." She took a moment to wipe away a tear of happiness drawn out by her husband's sincere words, and was gone. A minute later she was back and accompanied by Greg Blitzen. He was wearing the same white linen shirt and red bowtie ensemble he'd had on the first time they'd met; almost a year ago now.

"Good morning, Kris Kringle!" He exclaimed with cheer. "And a happy birthday to you!"

"You remembered. Thank you Greg."

"Of course, I did." Blitzen reached into his pocket, took out a sheet of paper, and handed it to him.

"What's this?"

"A list."

"Of what?"

"Of who has been mischievous and who has been good this year."

"I've no need of it. Graham already gave this to me a month ago."

"Yes well, like I once told you, it helps to check it twice."

"Right." Kris folded the paper in two and put it into his pocket.

"Listen, both of you," Greg started. "The main reason I'm here is to thank and congratulate you. And though I seemed absent this year I still looked in upon the operation with regularity. Honestly, I can't imagine how it could have gone any smoother. You've exceeded all expectations."

"That's good to hear," Kris said humbly.

"And even better to say."

"Are you here to watch the first flight tonight, Greg?" Cathy asked.

"Oh, no. I just came by to thank you and offer my best wishes for a successful night. I'm confident that Kris can take it from here."

"Will we see you again?"

"Oh yes, Cathy. This is just the beginning of many, many Christmas Eves for you two."

"Can you say exactly how many?" Kris queried.

"How many numbers can you count up to?"

"Quite a lot, Greg."

"Yes, well. That answer sounds about right. Let's go with "quite a lot."" He gave a chuckle and turned to go. "I'll see myself out. And once again, my sincerest gratitude to you both."

"To you too, Greg," Cathy answered.

Blitzen smiled once more, then walked out of the vestibule and out of sight.

"Some birthday, 'eh Cathy?"

"Kristopher, I think this is going to be your best one yet."

At eight o'clock that evening, a small group of Mechanic Elves brought the main sleigh out to a specially-manufactured runway that had never been used. At one end stood a recently constructed tent. It was enclosed on three sides, and had an awning in front large enough to fully cover the sleigh from the snow that was now coming down heavily. After pushing it under the shelter, the elves went quickly to work inspecting every inch of the vehicle for the last of dozens of times. They were making certain that no mechanical issues were overlooked and that everything was securely fastened.

Kris watched all of this through the bay window in the warm comfort of his parlor. The fireplace crackled familiarly as the flames once again consumed the logs of wood they'd been fed. He could see them reflecting brightly in the glass. Next to the fire was a ten-foot tall Christmas tree, a full Alaskan pine that he and Chuck had gone out and cut down themselves over three weeks back. It was adorned with strings of popcorn, cranberries, candy canes and glass ornaments, all hanging gaily from its branches. He could see its reflection, too. While the entire scene was both majestic and reminiscent of his early years in New England, his thoughts remained focused on that evening's task. His uncertainty had been growing all day, but he'd been careful not to show it. From behind him came a noise, and without looking he recognized it as the gentle footsteps of his wife.

"Almost ready, Nicky?" She asked sweetly. He continued staring out the window with his hands in his pockets.

"I'm not sure that I could be readier, Cathy. Though at times today I've wished that I could postpone this task indefinitely."

"No, you don't."

"No, I don't. You're right, of course." He looked at her and saw that she was carrying a large box wrapped in red paper, and with a single green bow affixed.

"What's this?"

"Open it and see." He took it from her and brought it over to his carving table. Kris unwrapped the paper and removed the cover from the box. "Oh my goodness, I almost forgot!" he exclaimed. "My uniform."

"Well sweetheart, you can't go out in that ragged linen shirt. The time has come at last for you to dress your part."

"That's true," he agreed. "Let's see what we have here." From the box he removed a heavy red jacket trimmed thickly in white and a dark forest green. The green was so dark, in fact, that from a short distance it could easily be mistaken for black. The pants were a match to the jacket, with the belt and boots the same dark forest green. To top it off was a red cap with a white brim folded up around its circumference. It had several inches of extra material resting over the side. Attached to its end was the white silk snowball Cathy had given him earlier that morning. The entire suit was perfect.

"Do you like it, Nicky?" She asked with a slight hesitation.

"It's perfect," he repeated his own thoughts out loud to her. "Thank you ever so much, honey." He paused and thought for a moment. "Well, I guess it's time to go put it on."

"I guess so." He put the suit back in the box and started to carry it up to their room. As he walked by her this time she kissed him on the cheek, and then watched him head up the stairs.

Santa Claus came downstairs fully dressed in his new uniform just after 8:30p.m. He walked through the kitchen and toward the doorway that led into his workshop. Before he could walk in though, he was intercepted by Cathy and Graham.

"Well, well, Kris Kringle, aren't you a sight," Graham pronounced with a chuckle. "Finally, we're not the only ones dressed like we jumped off of a cereal box."

"Cereal box?" Cathy asked, perplexed.

Kris didn't get the futuristic reference either, but he let it pass in favor of a sarcastic retort. "At least it's only once a year for me, old sprite."

"Bah!" he exclaimed. "So it is, human. Touché." Kris laughed heartily at the remark and then turned to Cathy. "Well?"

"Graham's right, you are indeed a sight to behold; a great one." She hugged him. "You take care of yourself out there tonight, Nicky. Be careful and come back to me in one piece."

"That'll be easy, sweetheart. The reindeer do most of the work."

"All of it, actually," Graham chimed in.

"Who asked you, anyway?" Kris returned with feigned annoyance.

"Listen you two. If you don't mind, it's time to get one of you out there and onto a sleigh."

Tears of happiness and pride rolled down Cathy's eyes as she looked upon her husband. She hugged him once more, and all three of them went into the workshop together. There was no work on

Christmas Eve so as on Thanksgiving every elf, save those few outside tending to the sleigh, was in attendance. Charlie stepped forward and extended his hand. Kris shook it. "Best to you out there tonight, Mr. Kringle. Uh, Mr. Claus."

"From me, too." It was William, who had just joined them. Kris shook his hand as well."

"All right gentleman, let's get on with it. Care to take a walk in the snow?"

"I thought you'd never ask," William answered.

Kris Kringle looked out over a sea of elves. After a quick glance at his watch he realized that he didn't have time for any long speeches.

"It's time, all," he said simply. "I'll see you in the morning." Kris gave them a smile and a wave and then went through the main door out into the driving snow. The handymen went with him. Cathy and Graham stayed behind and watched from the doorway.

"I hope it goes well, Graham. I really do." There was a tinge of apprehension in her voice, but she didn't care.

"He'll do exceptionally well, Cathy Sue Kringle," Graham said in a jolly, comforting voice.

The trio reached the semi-tent and saw that the reindeer had already been harnessed. They walked beneath the covered portion, where they were met by the full complement of Mechanic Elves.

"How's she look?" Kris shouted into the blustery wind.

"She's perfect, Santa; in great shape," the elf nearest him said. "Now remember, balance is the key. Just steer sir, the reindeer will do the rest. Speak your normal English; they'll understand your commands." Kris looked over to the back compartment of the sleigh. The gifts were overflowing; resting on top of them was an entirely full red cloth bag with a rope handle loop at its top.

"Are you sure all the presents are in there?" Kris asked skeptically.

"Yes. It's a lot more spacious than it looks," the elf shouted back to him. Then he winked. "Trust us."

"I guess I'll have to now." He then turned to his long-time friends. "Billy, Chuck; watch over things till I get back, all right?"

"You've got it, Mr. Kringle!" William exclaimed. Charlie simply nodded.

Kris pulled from his jacket pocket the storm goggles that Basil had given him earlier, yanked them over his cap, and adjusted them properly. "Okay, guys," he shouted out to the elves surrounding the sleigh, "move out, please!" They did as they were instructed. Kris Kringle then climbed into his sleigh and got comfortable. He moved his cap's overhanging white silken snowball to the right side so that it wasn't in his eyes, and then picked up the reins. "All right, let's get started." He gave the reins a quick shake, and slowly the reindeer pulled out from under the tent's awning with the sleigh trailing right behind them.

Without cover, the snow enveloped them immediately. Kris had no idea how he himself was going to see through the dynamic blizzard, let alone his team of caribou. Nevertheless, he carried on. Forty-five years ago this very night, Robert Donner had somehow found a way to navigate himself and his father through identical weather conditions. And Kris would find a way to get through them now.

As Cathy, Graham and the elves watched through the large factory windows, and William, Charlie and the Mechanic Elves looked on from twenty feet away, Kris gave the historic first command from the back of his sleigh. "On your marks now. Okay deer, ready?! Take us up…now!" Instantaneously the reindeer stepped forward in unison, and all nine, including Kris, moved out and up as one unit. In a flash they were in the air, elevating higher and higher as if they were actually trying to get above the snow. Up there against the backdrop of the moonlight the visibility was much clearer. Kris looked down at his friends, who were looking up and waving to him. He waved back and, though certain that they couldn't hear him, called out to them anyway. "Merry Christmas, Snowhenge!"

He now focused all of his attention on the reindeer in front of him. They were heading south from Alaska and through Canada to a territory that would one day be known, Graham had told him, as the state of Washington. Kris Kringle, who was born on the very eve of General George Washington's first major victory of the American Revolution in Trenton, New Jersey, thought it was a good omen. And the perfect place to start.

Santa Claus sat back with the reins, looked over below and to the right, and beheld the absolute majesty of the Arctic Ocean. Illuminated by the bright glow of the moonlight, it was truly an extraordinary sight. His trepidation had faded away entirely, and in its place was confidence. Kris was now certain that this night would end with great success and, in fact, would be the first of many a successful Christmas yet to come.

As it turned out, he was right.

# ACKNOWLEDGEMENT

There is no way to write this story without offering a word of gratitude to Clement Clarke Moore. The New York-native's 1823 poem, "A Visit from St. Nicholas", featured the famous names of St. Nick's eight reindeer, and steered the Santa Claus narrative in the direction that ultimately brought us to where we are with it today.

# ABOUT THE AUTHOR

Chris Gay is an author, freelance writer, voice-over artist, broadcaster and actor. He wrote the paranormal, theological thriller novel *Ghost of a Chance*, the novella *Sherlock Holmes and the Final Reveal* and several humor books: *And That's the Way It Was...Give or Take: A Daily Dose of My Radio Writings, The Bachelor Cookbook: Edible Meals with a Side of Sarcasm, Shouldn't Ice Cold Beer Be Frozen? My 365 Random Thoughts to Improve Your Life Not One Iota, Another Round of Ice Cold Beer: My 365 More Random Thoughts to Improve Your Life Not One Iota* and the upcoming *Something Witty This Way Comes*. For 7 years he wrote and broadcast a daily, sponsored radio humor spot in Hartford, Connecticut. He's been published nationally in *Writer's Digest*, written and voiced radio commercials, authored a variety of comedic, non-comedic content, sports articles, scripts, press releases, website, media and technical content. He's also acted in a couple of movies and plays. His website is *chrisjgay.com*.

www.ingramcontent.com/pod-product-compliance
Lightning Source LLC
Chambersburg PA
CBHW050832180626
46814CB00004B/1588